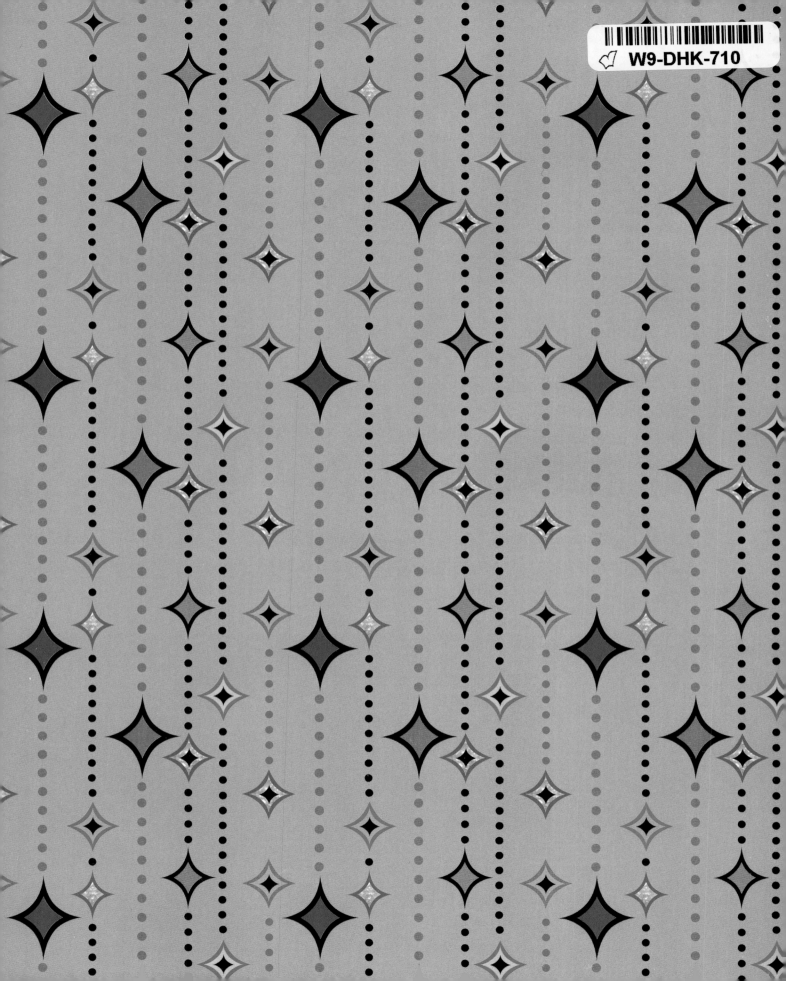

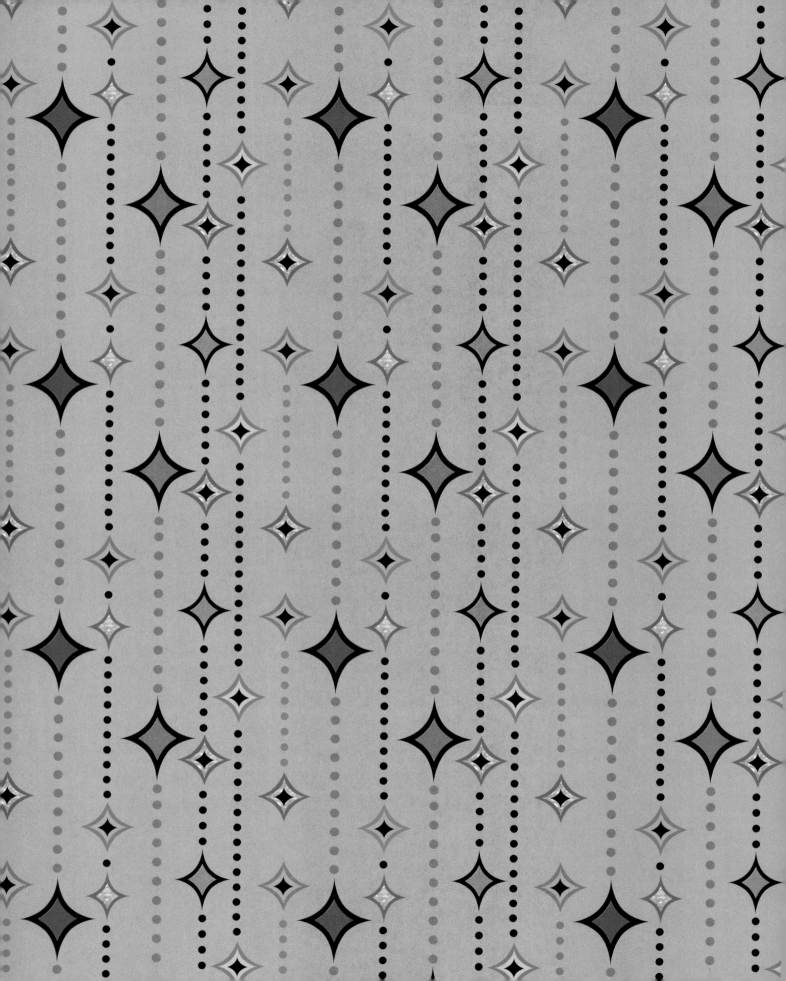

Monster Magic!

Adapted by Kristen L. Depken

Based on the teleplay "A Very Genie Halloweenie" by Whitney Fox

Illustrated by Dave Aikins

 A GOLDEN BOOK • NEW YORK

randomhousekids.com
ISBN 978-1-5247-1671-4
Printed in the United States of America
10 9 8 7 6 5 4 3 2 1

One day, Shimmer and Shine were in their kitchen decorating cakes.

"Frosting is my favorite part of cake!" said Shimmer, licking a spoon.

Just then, their bracelets started to glow.

"Shimmer and Shine, my genies divine, through this special chant, three wishes you'll grant," said a voice. It was their friend Leah!

"Your best friends are on the way!" Shimmer and Shine jumped onto their magic carpet and took off.

Poof! The genies appeared in Leah's living room . . . and landed inside a giant cauldron full of candy!

"I don't know what you're up to, Leah," said Shine, "but this night is off to a great start."

"It's Halloween! You guys are going trick-or-treating with me!" Leah announced.

Shimmer frowned. "But wait. People might see that we're genies."

Leah shook her head. "That's what's great about Halloween. No one will know you're *real* genies. They'll just think you're wearing genie costumes!" She handed each of them a jack-o'-lantern pail for collecting candy. "C'mon, guys. Let's trick-or-treat at Zac's house first!"

When the friends arrived at Zac's, he was dressed up as a spider attached to a web.

"I got a little crazy with the glue, and now I'm stuck," he explained. "It happens. Happens a lot."

Shimmer, Shine, and Leah pulled Zac down. Leah introduced him to the genies.

"Those are some great genie costumes!" said Zac.

Zac was excited to show Leah and the genies his haunted-house creations. He pointed to a graveyard filled with boxes. "Here lie the tombstones of *haunted*-licious . . . pizzas!" He continued the tour, bringing his friends over to a large kitchen pot. "And here is the witches' cauldron, for brewing magical potions and . . . bobbing for apples!" But Zac didn't have any apples, so he had filled the pot with potatoes.

Zac had even put a mask on his dog's face, turning Rocket into the scariest werewolf ever! But he had saved his spookiest surprise for last.

"Prepare yourselves! The monster that lies ahead is sure to spook you out of your socks!" he warned.

"Behold . . . Frankenstein!" Zac shined his flashlight on a figure in the corner. "I borrowed my grandma's plastic Santa and painted it green."

Leah and the genies were impressed.

"I hope it's enough to win the Best Haunted House contest," Zac said. "But just to make sure, I'm going to check out the other houses." He wished Leah, Shimmer, and Shine a happy Halloween, then headed down the street.

Zac didn't realize that as he left, he bumped into a stack of jack-o'-lanterns. They toppled to the ground and rolled across the yard, knocking into the other decorations and ruining his haunted house!

"Oh, no!" cried Leah. "He worked so hard to get
ready for the contest. If only we could help him."
Shimmer smiled. "You can make a wish!"

"For my first wish," said Leah, "I wish for Zac's house to be decorated!"

"Boom, Zahramay! First wish of the day!" Shimmer used her genie magic to decorate Zac's house—like a big birthday cake.

"I wanted it to be spooky," said Leah, "not yummy."

"Oh, candy corns," said Shimmer. "My mistake."

Leah used her second wish to fix Shimmer's mistake.
"I wish Zac had a real haunted house."

"*Boom, Zahramay!*" said Shine. "*Second wish of the day!*" She turned the cake decorations into spiderwebs, skeletons, bats, and other super-spooky objects.

"Now, *this* is more like it!" said Leah. "Zac's definitely
going to win the haunted-house contest now."
"Especially with the monster!" exclaimed Shine.
"What monster?" asked Leah nervously.

"The one right behind you!" yelled Shine.

A huge Frankenstein monster emerged from the shadows! The friends hid in a giant cauldron. The monster groaned and started walking toward them!

"Why is a real, live, walking and moaning Frankenstein coming out of Zac's house?" Leah asked.

"You wanted a real haunted house, so I gave you
a real monster," Shine said.

"I wanted Zac's house to *look* haunted, not *be*
haunted!" said Leah.

"My mistake, Leah," said Shine.

"It's okay, Shine," said Leah. "Mistakes happen. We just have to figure out what to do so Frankenstein doesn't find us."

Shimmer snapped her fingers. "I've got it! Maybe he won't see us if we don't move."

Shine shook her head as the monster came closer. "Nope. He sees us."

The monster marched around the yard, stomping on pumpkins and laughing at the squishy sound they made.

"Hey, Frankenstein's not scary!" Leah smiled. "He's actually kind of adorable."

Frankenstein beamed.

"Hi! Me Frankenstein," the monster said.

"This is awesome!" said Leah. "Zac's got a great shot at winning the haunted-house contest now."

"Yeah! He's got a real monster, and spiderwebs, and fog. . . ." Shine started to cough. "Well, maybe a little too much fog."

"I gotcha covered, sis!" said Shimmer. She conjured a handheld vacuum cleaner and sucked the fog out of the air. "There! The fog is all gone."

Shine gasped. "And so is Frank!"

The girls looked to see where the monster was. He was halfway down the street, stomping on more pumpkins! "Ooooh. Lots of squishies," Frankenstein giggled. "Squish! Squish! Squish!"

"We have to get him back before anybody realizes he's a real monster!" said Leah. She and the genies ran down the street in search of Frankenstein, but all they found was a monster mess.

Then Leah noticed piles of squished
pumpkins with giant footprints in them.
"Frankenstein left a trail!" she exclaimed.
"If we follow it, we'll find him."

The girls followed Frankenstein's messy trail.
"Wait," Leah said after they had passed a
bunch of squished pumpkins and overturned
trash cans. "We can't just leave everything like
this. We have to clean up Frank's monster mess."

"I was hoping you'd say that!" said Shimmer. She made her handheld vacuum appear once again. "I love cleaning!"

The friends worked together to restore Zac's neighborhood.

Soon the neighborhood was clean again, and everyone's spooky decorations were back in place.

"Guys, look!" cried Leah.

"At how nice the place looks?" Shimmer nodded proudly. "I know. It's beautiful."

"Well, it is beautiful, but I mean look over there! It's Frank!"

The giant monster was heading down the street! Shine tried to stop him, but he wanted to keep smashing pumpkins.

"Frank see more squishies!" he giggled.

"I wish we could just stop Frankenstein!" said Leah.

"Boom, Zahramay! Third wish of the day!" chanted Shimmer. *"Shimmer and Shine, stop Frankenstein divine!"*

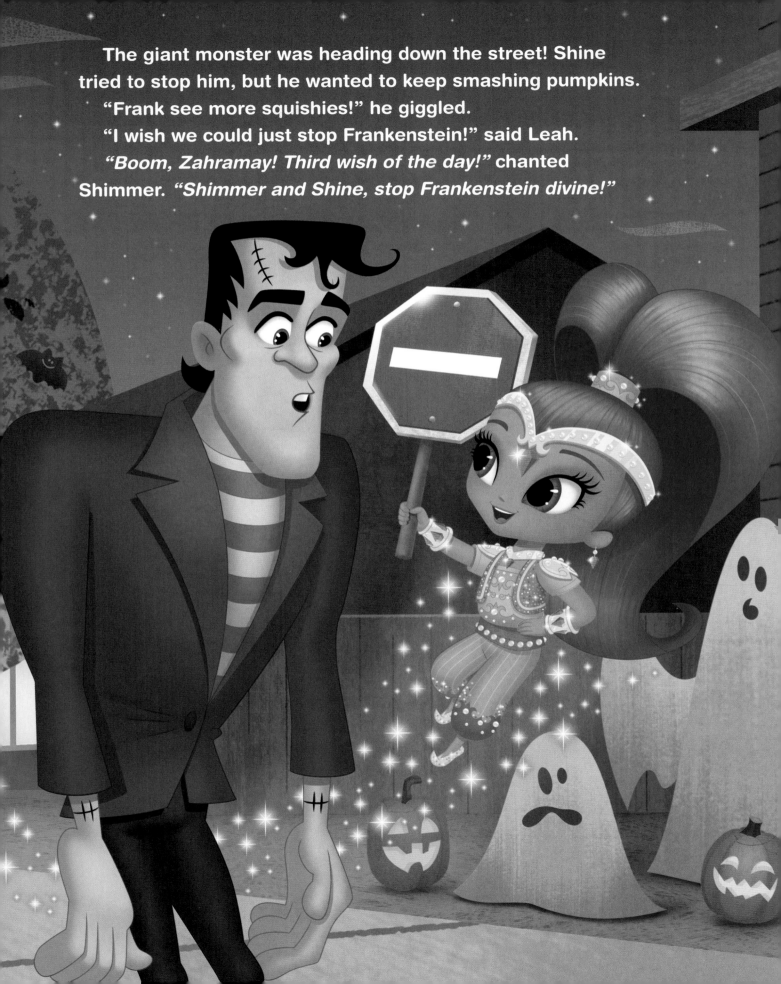

"That's my last wish!" cried Leah. She hadn't meant to make her third wish. But it was too late. Shimmer used her magic to create a giant, sticky web.

"Uh, Shimmer, what is that?" asked Leah.

"A way to stop Frank!" Shimmer grinned. "Just like you wished for."

Leah shook her head. "But there's no way a spiderweb is gonna stop a guy with monster muscles."

"Oopsie! Since it stopped Zac, I thought it would work
on Frank." Shimmer hung her head. "My mistake."
"Actually, it was my mistake for making the wish,"
Leah told the genie. "But we can't let it stop us. Even if
we don't have a way to stop Frankenstein."

Leah hoped she was wrong, and that the magical spiderweb would catch the massive monster. But Frankenstein walked through the web as though it were cotton candy!

Just then, Frankenstein noticed that a spider from Shimmer's web was on his shoulder. He jumped up and down in terror.

"Frank no like spiders!" he cried.

"It's okay, Frank," said Shine, flying over to the monster.
"You don't need to be scared of this little guy. He's nice."
Frankenstein stopped. "Spider is friend?" he asked.
"Shimmer, your mistake worked!" said Leah. "You got
Frankenstein to stop!" Then she had an idea. "Maybe we can
use the spider to get Frank to follow us back to Zac's house."

Leah's plan worked! A few moments later, Frankenstein was safely back at Zac's house. He even played with his new spider friend.

"I might not know how to explain Frankenstein to Zac," laughed Leah, "but I'm still glad he's here."

Suddenly, Zac ran up the street with a trophy in his hand. "I won the Best Haunted House contest!" he said excitedly.

"That's great, Zac!" Leah said, congratulating her friend.

Zac grinned from ear to ear. "Yeah, they said I had the best monster on the street!"

Then Zac saw Frankenstein. "Whoa! I don't remember my green Santa looking like this!" He shrugged. "But it's Halloween. Spooky things happen. A lot. Come on, Frank! Let's pass out some candy."

When Zac and Frankenstein were gone, Leah thanked
Shimmer and Shine for their help. "Even with the mistakes
we made today, this was my favorite Halloween ever!"
"Mine too!" said Shimmer. "We got to meet Frankenstein
and decorate. We are two lucky genies."

Leah hugged the two genies as they got ready to go home. "We fixed our mistakes, and our day turned out great!"

"Boom, Zahramay!" Shimmer and Shine hopped onto their magic carpet and soared off, counting down the days until the next Halloween.

Back in Zahramay Falls, Shimmer and Shine finished decorating
their cake. Lucky for them, they had one more pair of hands to help!

"Frank all done!" announced Frankenstein as he revealed his
creation: a giant pumpkin-shaped cake.

Shine took a bite. "Well, Shimmer, you were right. Frosting really
is the best part of cake!"

The friendly monster took a giant bite of his cake. He thought
the frosting was the best part, too!

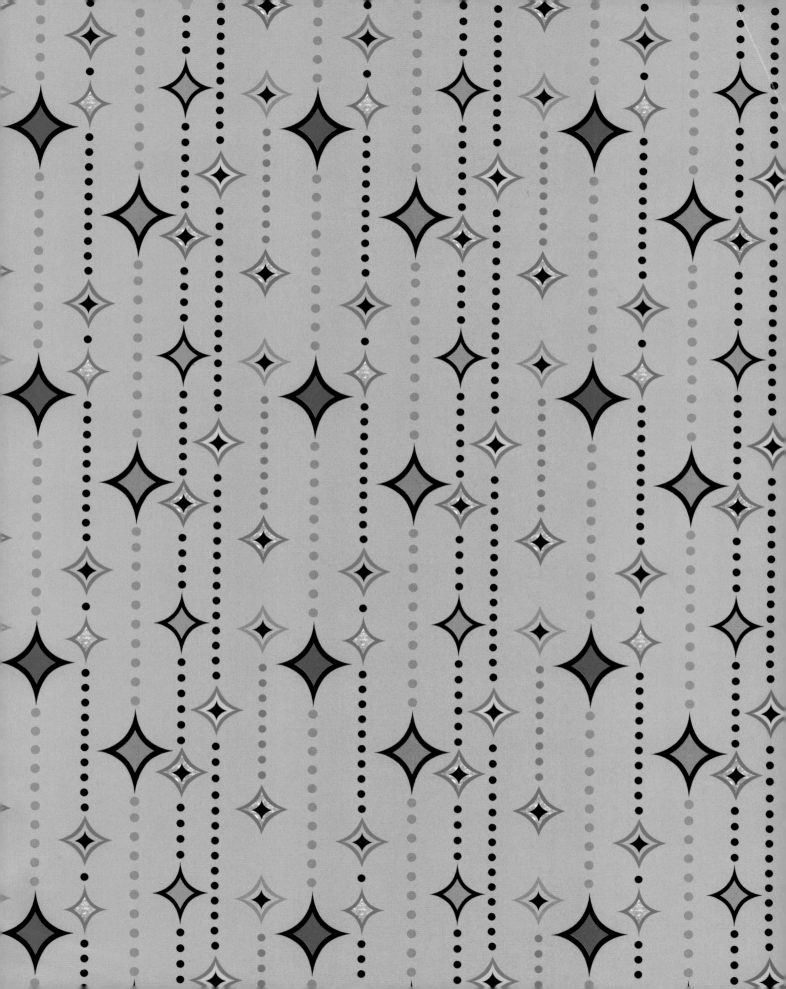

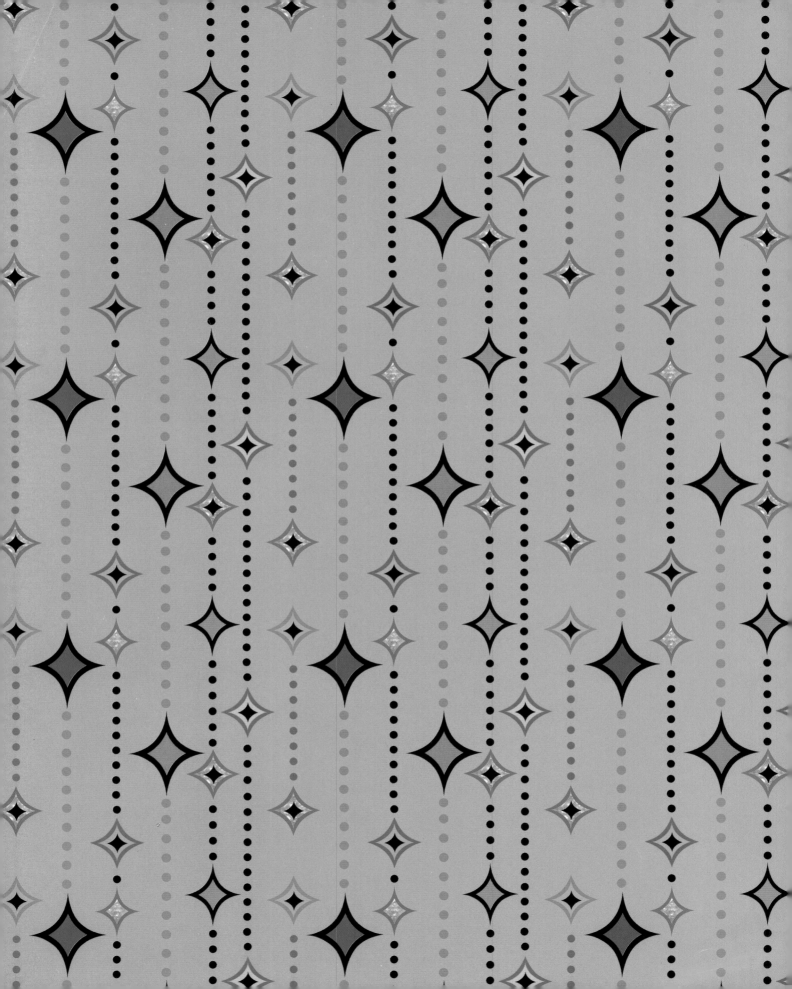